HAPPY BIRTHDAY, MOON

FRANK ASCH

ALADDIN PAPERBACKS

Aladdin Paperbacks
An imprint of Simon & Schuster
Children's Publishing Division
1230 Avenue of the Americas
New York, New York 10020

Revised cover edition, 1999
Also available in a hardcover edition from Simon & Schuster
Books for Young Readers
8 10 9 7

Library of Congress Cataloging-in-Publication Data
Asch, Frank   Happy birthday, moon.
Summary: When a bear discovers
that the moon shares his birthday,
he buys the moon a beautiful hat as a present.
[1. Bears—Fiction. 2. Moon—Fiction.
3. Birthdays—Fiction]. I. Title.
[PZ7.A778Hap 1988] [E] 88-6569

ISBN 0-689-83544-2

To Devin

One night Bear looked up at the sky
and thought, wouldn't it be nice
to give the moon a birthday present.

But Bear didn't know when the moon's
birthday was, or what to get him.
So he climbed a tall tree to have
a little chat with the moon.
"Hello, Moon!" he shouted.
But the moon did not reply.
Maybe I am too far away, thought Bear,
and the moon cannot hear me.

So Bear paddled across the river...

and hiked through the forest…

into the mountains.

Now I am much closer to the moon,
thought Bear, and again he shouted:
"Hello!"
This time his own voice echoed
off one of the other mountains:
"Hello!"
Bear got very excited.
Oh, boy! he thought,
I'm talking to the moon.
"Tell me," asked Bear,
"when is your birthday?"
"Tell me, when is your birthday?"
replied the moon.

"Well, it just so happens that
  my birthday is tomorrow!" said Bear.
"Well, it just so happens that
  my birthday is tomorrow!" said the moon.
"What do you want for your birthday?"
  asked Bear.
"What do you want for your birthday?"
  asked the moon.
  Bear thought for a moment, then he replied:
"I would like a hat."
"I would like a hat," said the moon.
  Oh, goody! thought Bear, now I know
  what to get the moon for his birthday.

"Goodbye," said Bear.
"Goodbye," said the moon.

When Bear got home, he dumped all the money out of his piggy bank.

Then he went downtown...

and bought the moon a beautiful hat.

That night he put the hat up in a tree
where the moon could find it. Then he
waited and watched while the moon slowly

crept up through the branches and
tried on the hat.
"Hurray!" yelled Bear. "It fits just right!"

During the night while Bear slept, the hat fell
out of the tree. In the morning Bear
found the hat on his doorstep.
"So the moon got me a hat, too!" exclaimed Bear.
He tried it on and it fit perfectly.

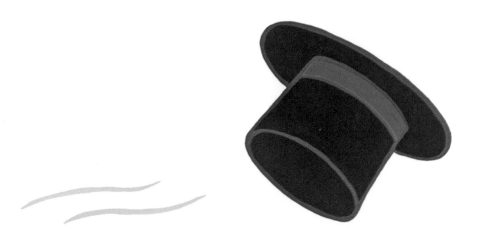

But just then, the wind blew Bear's hat
off his head. He chased after it...

but it got away.

That night Bear paddled across the river...

and hiked through the forest…

to talk with the moon.

For a long time the moon would
  not speak to him, so Bear spoke first.
"Hello!" he shouted.
"Hello!" replied the moon.
"I lost the beautiful hat you gave me,"
  said Bear.
"I lost the beautiful hat you gave me,"
  said the moon.
"That's okay, I still love you!"
  said Bear.
"That's okay, I still love you!"
  said the moon.

"HAPPY BIRTHDAY!" said Bear.
"HAPPY BIRTHDAY!" said the moon.